The Christmas Tree Moose

By Lisa Soland

With illustrations
by Samuel Jack

Climbing Angel Publishing
KNOXVILLE, TENNESSEE

THE CHRISTMAS TREE MOOSE
Written by Lisa Soland
Illustrated by Samuel Jack

Text copyright © 2014 Lisa Soland
Illustrations copyright © 2024 Lisa Soland

Sequel to *The Christmas Tree Angel*

Climbing Angel Publishing
PO Box 32381, Knoxville, Tennessee 37930
www.ClimbingAngel.com

Published in December 2024
Printed in the United States of America
Book design by Climbing Angel Publishing

ISBN: 978-1-956218-44-2
Library of Congress Control Number: 2024925803

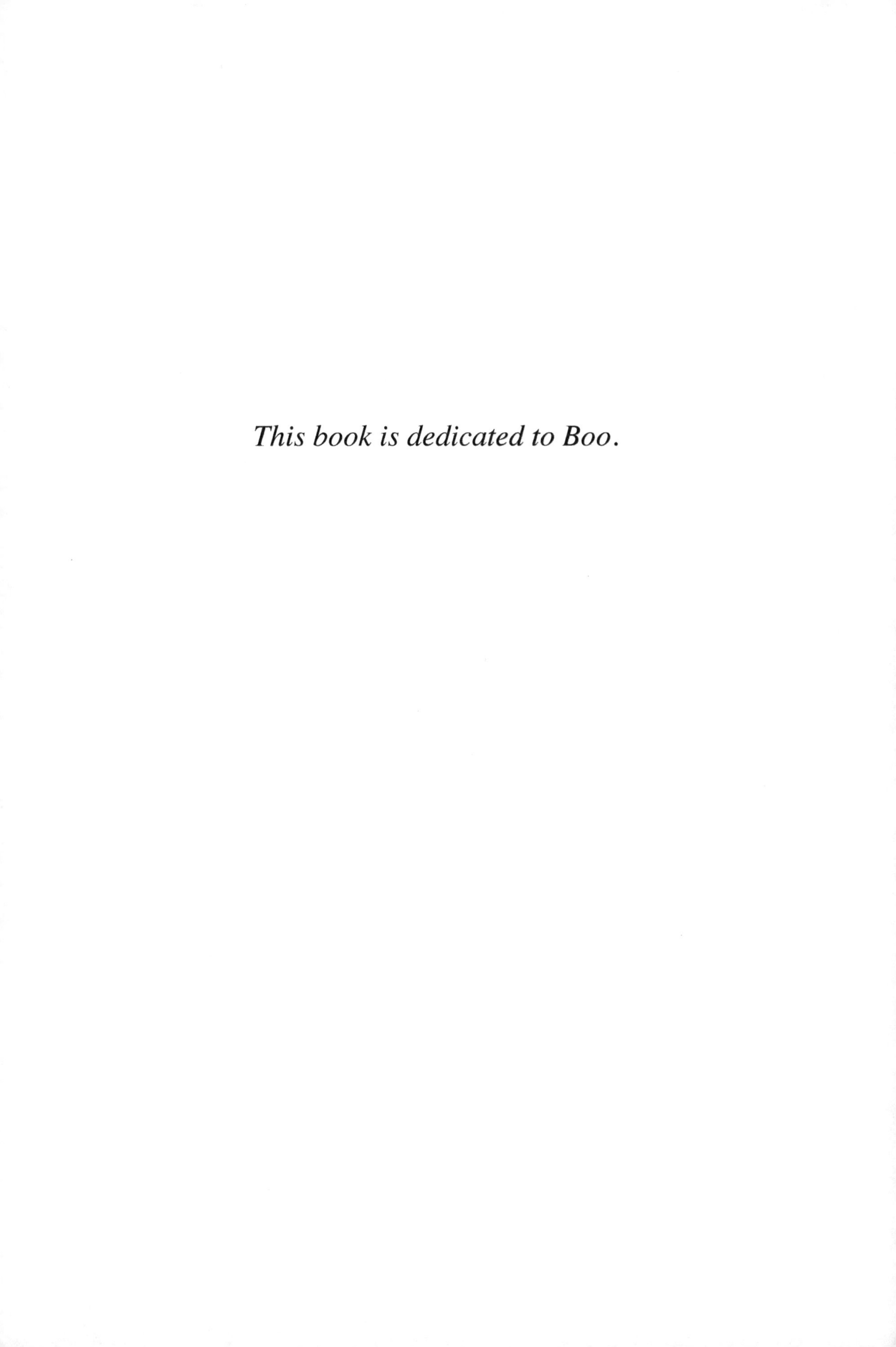

This book is dedicated to Boo.

The Christmas Tree Moose

Chapter 1

Circumstances

The moose saw no reason whatsoever to get himself out of the basket in which he lived. *Today is the same as yesterday, and tomorrow will prove to be no different*, he thought. Besides, things were fine. His needs were met. There was the warm blanket and plenty of room to lie down whenever he felt the need to do so.

There was no reason to leave except that the basket was located in Mrs. Brown's sewing room, and she rarely ever visited, which made the moose very lonely.

His unpromising circumstances convinced him that he had no choice in the matter. Things were as they were, after all. He was an unmade moose, and being unmade limited his ability to change his circumstances.

He placed his head upon his arm, which was propped up on the edge of his hand-woven home. He watched out the window as the night before Christmas Eve ended with a freezing rain. Soaked particles fell from the gray-streaked sky as the sun disappeared below the horizon.

Changes in the weather lifted his spirits. Any change pleased the moose because he had come to expect no change at all.

"December is my favorite month," he declared aloud to no one in particular because no one was there to listen. But this did not keep the moose from sharing. He expressed his thoughts continuously as if the floorboards had ears.

The moose chuckled, imagining the corners of the wood pealed up and just beneath the edges, ears popping out to receive all the creativity that he had to offer. It thrilled him to think that something or someone listened to his mental wanderings and outlandish imagination. This is one thing that worked in his favor. His circumstances allowed him lots of time to think.

The moose harbored one thought, though, that was not particularly creative or imaginative. It repeated itself over and over again, simple and straightforward: *If I do today what I did yesterday and the day before, chances are very good that I will do it again tomorrow.* This thought dominated the space inside his head. He felt as if he were one of Mrs. Brown's snow globes shaken up. All those snow particles scattered about, yet still contained, with nothing ever really changing.

Some days, he sat motionless so the particles in his head would not dance around, reminding him of his unchanging situation. But simply opening his eyes in the morning stirred the snow, and those straightforward, unavoidable thoughts would swirl.

Chapter 2

The Gift of Smell

The moose clung to the simple changes of night to day and back
again. His eyesight was not the best, so he preferred daytime
because he could see better. He also enjoyed the aromas as Mrs.
Brown prepared the meals for her son, Tommy, and her husband,
Mr. Brown. Of all the moose's senses, his sense of smell served
him best. Besides the changes between night and day and
variations in the weather, smells had the most significant impact on
his daily life.

This particular morning, Mrs. Brown had served porridge with
raisins and maple syrup, along with coffee. It was delightful. For
the noon meal, there likely wouldn't be much to sniff; probably
soup. However, the aromas from dinner were overwhelming. He
guessed the meat might be pork, but he was certain about the peas
because one of them had rolled away after prayer time.

"Come, Lord Jesus, be our guest. Let these gifts to us be
blessed. Amen," and down the hallway, the pea rolled and stopped
right in front of the doorway to the sewing room.

The moose longed to jump out of the basket and retrieve it.
"What an outlandish idea," he realized. "I've never been out of this
basket. What makes me think I could climb out now, pick up that
pea, and deliver it safely back to the kitchen table? I must be losing
my mind," he concluded.

His ideas were unique, but that's what you get from a life of isolation and only being able to watch the rain fall as your primary form of entertainment. "Isolation might be good for forming ideas. But fellowship, time spent with others, must be good for something more meaningful," he said. But for what, the moose did not know.

He listened intently to the voices from the hall and imagined where each of the Browns sat at the kitchen table. Mr. Brown probably sat at the head, and he pictured Mrs. Brown and Tommy sitting across from one another. Perhaps Mrs. Brown sat the closest to the oven so she could dish out the food as needed.

She always moved about, carrying things from here to there. Sure, Mr. Brown fetched the wood from the wintry outdoors and piled it by the front door, but Mrs. Brown distributed the logs to the kitchen and bedrooms.

With no fireplace in the sewing room, the moose was grateful for his soft blanket. He wrapped it around himself just right, leaving a small portion loose to use as a pillow.

The moose knew Mrs. Brown best because she was home almost every day, all day. He felt closest to her, but as hard as he tried, he could not understand why she couldn't sew on his other leg. Tommy had two legs, as did Mrs. Brown and Mr. Brown, but the moose only had one, which is why he never tried to get out of his basket. *It isn't a matter of courage*, he thought. It is simply a matter of balance.

"Can't we decorate the tree tonight, Mom?" the moose heard Tommy ask.

"School tomorrow. It's time for you to go to bed," said Mrs. Brown.

"Ohhhhh, gosh. I'm not a bit tired."

"Off you go, young man," said Mr. Brown.

Tommy kissed his mother and then his father and ran down the hall past the room where the moose lived. His bare foot stepped squarely on top of the green pea still sitting in the hall outside the sewing room door.

"Ewww. Yuck," said Tommy.

"What, dear?"

"It's a pea from dinner. I stepped on it."

"It isn't going to kill you," said his mother.

"It's stuck."

"Bring it here."

Tommy tried to wipe the smashed vegetable off with his hand. "It won't come off!"

"Come here," said his mother.

Tommy hopped on one leg back to the kitchen, and after only a moment or two, he ran happily down the hall to the room where he slept.

"I'll tuck you in shortly," called his father from the table.

The moose slept when Tommy slept because Mr. Brown blew out the light in the hall. He would do a little more thinking in the dark, and then, like all nights leading up to this one, the moose would shut his eyes and fall asleep. That night, he dreamt about hopping on one leg, like Tommy.

Chapter 3

Change

The next morning, Tommy searched for something in the window box and, not finding it there, slammed the lid shut, waking the moose.

"I can't find it, Mother."

"Well, I don't know what to tell you," cried Mrs. Brown. "You will not leave this house without a hat."

Mrs. Brown wore her Christmas apron with the bright red poinsettias decorating the edges. She walked firmly into the room where the moose lived, crossed to the basket where he sat, reached down into his home, and pulled out his green blanket. One moment keeping him warm, the next moment, gone, as quickly as that! Radical change was suddenly thrust upon him. The moose would have to learn to do without. He was left with nothing but a thin cotton fabric beneath him. He used this to keep his bottom from itching.

"Tommy. Get your shoes on, or you won't get those papers delivered in time, and you'll be late for school."

"I can't find my hat, Mom!"

"I'm taking care of the hat. Get your shoes on and your galoshes. It's wet outside."

Mrs. Brown pulled out the antique chair tucked beneath the sewing table, sat down, and opened one of its drawers. She removed two long, slender pieces of wood, each with a knob on the end. Arranging the sticks in her hands, she slipped their pointed tops together back and forth, quickly changing the shape of the moose's blanket, then called to her son, "Tommy! You'll be late!"

He came running with his shoes laced and his lunch bag in hand. "No, I won't. Mrs. Weber waits for me when I'm not there."

Mrs. Brown pulled the moose's blanket up and over Tommy's head. It made a perfect hat. "Well, we don't want teachers waiting for us, do we? We should be where we're supposed to be when we're supposed to be there."

Tommy nodded his head, having heard this instruction many times. "Off you go." She patted his bottom, and he ran for the front door.

Eight was an important year for Tommy. He had begun to remember the directions his mother and father gave him. This made life easier. As he grew more responsible, his parents became more proud of him, which pleased Tommy.

Being able to hold more things in his head, though, meant that other things had to go. Tommy sensed the changes taking place but could not always put his finger on them. Mrs. Brown watched him from the window as he loaded the newspapers into the basket on his red bike.

To make room for the thick Christmas edition of the Sun Valley Times, Tommy had to remove the angel and the soldier ornaments from their home in the basket. He ran back to the house and pulled open the front door.

"Mom! The angel and the soldier won't fit anymore. What should I do with them?"

"Don't walk on my clean floors!" called Mrs. Brown. "Set them there by the fireplace, and I'll place them on your dresser."

Tommy did as his mother instructed, mounted his bike, and descended the hill from where the Brown family home stood.

Just then, the teakettle sounded off, loud and strong, whistling a pitch that could not be ignored. Mrs. Brown tossed the two wooden sticks into the moose's home and ran toward the kitchen.

"Well, what do we have here?" asked the moose. He wrapped his arms around the two sticks and tried to move them off to one side. "I lost my warm blanket and gained these two useless sticks."

Although disappointed with the trade-off, he remained grateful for his thick pants and plaid wool jacket. But without the blanket, he worried these clothes might not be enough to keep him warm during the night. Through the window, he felt the sun shining brightly onto his little home. "Thank God," he said. "Thank God for these little miracles."

Chapter 4

Garland

The moose heard Mrs. Brown wash the breakfast dishes, dry them, and place them back into the cabinet. He then heard popping sounds, like the sound of a cap gun. This is a sound he normally heard in the evening hours, so hearing them now, after breakfast, disoriented him.

Before his imagination could get the better of him, Mrs. Brown entered the sewing room carrying a ceramic bowl filled with puffed-up snowflakes.

"I better get this popcorn strung before Tommy gets home from school," she said to herself. Otherwise, he'll insist on doing it, and there'll be another mess to clean up." She sat on the antique chair, sighed, and then opened one of the drawers to the sewing table.

Mrs. Brown removed a tiny, sharp object and pulled a piece of white rope through its top. She then licked the tips of her fingers and tied a knot in the rope's end.

"Oh, the cranberries!" she exclaimed.

She jumped up, left the room, and soon returned with yet another bowl. *They must be the cranberries*, thought the moose. They looked like peas, though, round in shape but larger and a dull red color instead of bright green.

The moose imagined the cranberries lined up next to the peas and thought these colors were especially nice side by side. But that must not have been the plan because Mrs. Brown stuck the popcorn with the needle and pulled the rope through, repeating this action ten times or more. Then she added a single cranberry. Then, ten more popcorns and one more cranberry. On and on she went. How beautiful!

As she strung, she sang. The moose pretended she sang to him. "Lo, how the Rose e'er blooming from tender stem hath sprung. Of Jesse's lineage coming, as men of old have sung."

She worked less urgently with Tommy away at school and Mr. Brown at his office. "It came, a flow'ret bright, amid the cold of winter, when half-spent was the night." She hummed quietly as she licked her fingers and formed another knot on the other end of the string then laid the new object on the floor.

The moose thought it was marvelous the way Mrs. Brown took three separate things—the popcorn, the rope and the cranberries and formed something brand new with them, something that did not exist before today. "This will look beautiful on the tree," she said, then sang some more, "To show God's love aright, she bore to men a Savior, when half-spent was the night." He didn't understand what she was singing about, but her passion told him that it must be something very important.

How delightful to have company, the moose thought. He couldn't remember the last time Mrs. Brown had sat beside him and pushed the sharp object with the rope through anything. She was so quick he wondered again why she didn't just quickly sew him a second leg.

She must have been the one to sew his plaid jacket and thick pants, so why not a leg? She had all the tools. She had the sharp object. She had the rope. There was plenty of cloth lying about the room. Why not a leg? He kept asking himself in the snow globe of his own tumbled-up mind, *Why not?*

Tommy had lost his hat, and Mrs. Brown quickly formed a new

one out of the moose's soft blanket. She easily created this strand of popcorn and cranberries to use for something special. But when it came to his missing leg, the world made no sense. Why wasn't he given two legs in the first place?

But he had waited this long. It wasn't going to hurt him to wait some more. And besides, what choice did he have? *No choice at all*, he thought.

Chapter 5

A Good Imagination

Mrs. Brown gathered the popcorn string and brought it into the living room, carefully placing it across the wingback chair. Then, as promised, she carried the angel and soldier ornaments into Tommy's room and gently set them on his dresser.

The moose felt a cool breeze when Mrs. Brown left the room. He scooted over to the edge of the basket, pulled the thin cotton fabric out from beneath him, and wrapped it around his body. He quickly remembered why he had been sitting on the material. The floor of the basket made his bottom itch, so he scratched it. Over and over, he scratched it. He wondered which was worse, the cool breeze left by an absent friend or the annoying willow bark that scraped his hindquarters. He thought maybe if he sat still, it would stop itching, but it didn't.

The moose decided it was time for him to stand on his one leg. Using the edge of the basket, he pulled himself up. It wasn't as difficult as he imagined. He remembered last night when Tommy stepped on the runaway pea and hopped back to the kitchen. The moose wondered if he, too, could hop on one leg like Tommy.

Mrs. Brown, busy baking in the kitchen, created the moose's favorite smells of all. She carved the apples, rolled out the pastry shells, laid them in her glass dishes, poured in the chunky cinnamon filling, added a second pastry on top, fluted the edges, poked them with a fork, and placed the three apple pies into the oven. All the while, the moose thought about hopping.

He sat back down and lifted his leg into the sky, bent it, and stretched it out again. "It seems to work just fine," he said. "What do I have to lose in trying?" He pulled himself up again and, holding onto the edge of the basket, took a deep breath. But he didn't jump. He started to hiccup instead. And then he hiccupped some more.

The moose didn't think he was afraid. Maybe he hesitated because jumping was something new to him. And since this didn't seem like a good enough reason not to do something, he held on to the edge of the basket and lifted himself off the ground. After a brief moment of suspension in empty space, he landed in the exact same place. "That wasn't so hard," he exclaimed. The hiccups were gone.

The clock in the hall chimed three as the moose continued to practice this jumping movement. He went up and down and up and down, exploring different positions and becoming quite bold.

All this action warmed him up and he no longer needed the cotton blanket, or any blanket at all, for that matter.

"Amazing. I could have jumped all along, and I never knew it," said the moose. As his excitement grew, he wondered what else he could do. A smile grew on his face that would not go away.

Chapter 6

Freedom

"**Y**o-ho-ho and a very merry Christmas!" yelled Tommy as he burst through the front door.

Mrs. Brown greeted him. "Well, what do we have here?"

"A pirate! Billy gave him to me. Isn't it something? He's got a patch over his eye and everything." After a pause, Tommy asked, "What's a pirate, mother?"

"I'm sure each pirate is unique, but for the most part, they ride around in big ships on the sea and frighten people."

"Why do they frighten people? What would be the purpose of that?"

"I'm not sure, Tommy. I suppose they think if they can make people afraid, they'll be able to take their treasure chests filled with valuable things."

"Like gold and silver?"

"I suppose."

Tommy struck a pose similar to that of the new ornament. He placed his fists on his hips and chanted, "Yo-ho-ho and a very happy New Year."

"Well, a very happy New Year to you, too."

"Billy's mom bought him at the store, and he's *imported.* What's *imported* mean?"

"It means that the ornament comes from another country."

"Boy, that's neat. All ours are just made here."

"Now, Tommy, there's not a thing wrong with something being made here." She helped him out of his wool coat and rubber boots.

"So, what do you think, Mom? Can we put him on the tree?"

"I don't see why not." She hung Tommy's coat in the hall closet.

Tommy ran to the tree and was about to place the small ornament on it when Mrs. Brown reminded him of his afternoon snack in the kitchen.

He spotted the popcorn and cranberry garland lying over the chair. "Oh, you made it without me," he said disappointedly, then tried to pick it up.

"Go drink your milk in the kitchen, and we'll decorate the tree," said Mrs. Brown.

Tommy headed for the kitchen and passed by the room with the moose. "Hi, Moose," he said. The moose stared at him directly.

It was jarring being said hello to out of the blue like that. Tommy had never spoken to the moose before. Why now? The moose remembered that he stood and jumped when Tommy walked by the door. Could Tommy have seen him jump? It all happened so fast that the moose couldn't think straight. Change had finally arrived, and it arrived so quickly that it was hard for the moose to hold an old thought in his head.

The moose wondered if the changes would keep coming. He thought about the strand of popcorn and cranberries and how Mrs. Brown pushed and pulled the rope through them. "Maybe changes can line up like that, too," said the moose. "One change happening right after the other."

"What might the next *change* be?" he wondered. "Could I jump out of this basket?" And as he thought it, the hiccups returned, but he went and did it anyway. He held on to the edge of the basket, pushed himself up into the air, and tumbled to the floor outside his home.

As he lay on the cold, hardwood floor, he looked around the room and realized how different life looked from this perspective. After all this time, he'd escaped the basket. The moose was finally free.

Chapter 7

Dry Needles

"**C**an I bring my treat in there, Mom?" yelled Tommy from the kitchen.

"Sure," she called back. "It is Christmas Eve, after all."

Tommy walked as fast as he could without spilling his milk. The white liquid rolled back and forth with each step. He held the soft cookie in his mouth, chewing as he spoke. "Caan I uut uh popcorn on uh three?"

"Chew your food first, Tommy…"

"'Before I speak.' I remember, Mom."

As he chewed, he tried to lift the long, delicate garland.

"It's wobbly. Maybe we better put this on together." He set the big glass of milk atop the round table and clapped his hands together with excitement. "Can you help me, Mom?"

"Of course."

Tommy picked up one end of the garland and Mrs. Brown the other, and together, they placed it onto the branches. Pine needles fell soundlessly to the hardwood floor.

"Look, Mom. Did you see that? Needles fell out."

"That's not good. Let me see." Mrs. Brown checked if the tree was in need of water but the pan below held plenty.

"Where should the pirate go?" Tommy asked as he held the new ornament up to the middle of the tree."

"That looks like as good a place as any."

"Is this all of them? It looks like we're missing some."

"What we don't have is your angel and the soldier. They're on your dresser," said Mrs. Brown. She smiled and began to hang the red and white candy canes on the tree.

Tommy filled his mouth with milk and, before swallowing, ran down the hall. As he passed by the sewing room, he turned his head to glance inside and then swallowed hard. "Holy cow. Where are you going?" He walked into the dimly lit room and over to the sewing basket.

The moose froze.

"Aren't you supposed to be in your basket?" Tommy bent down and picked up the moose, lifting him to eye level to take a good look. "Hi, Moose."

The moose smiled. But of course, he'd been smiling since this morning when all these changes began, and now the smile seemed permanently fixed on his face.

"What are you up to?" asked Tommy.

The moose wanted to say *"nothing"* because it seemed like the easiest way to break the ice between them, but *nothing* was the furthest thing from the truth. The moose thought about saying *"everything,"* but that suggested an awful lot, and it might frighten the boy. The moose got the hiccups again, but he stifled them for the time being.

"How 'bout I set you down here on Mom's sewing chair?"

How 'bout you bring me into the living room so I can watch you and your mom decorate this so-called Christmas tree? The moose thought those words, but they did not leave his mouth. They couldn't. Otherwise, the hiccups would pop out too. But he did imagine Tommy playing with him by the tree, surrounded by all the festivities and fun.

But in reality, Tommy placed the moose in the chair and carefully extended his leg out in front of him. "Mom!" he yelled.

"Yes, Tommy."

"Why haven't you finished making this moose?"

"I haven't had the time, son."

"I'd like to play with him. Couldn't you finish him?"

"Yes. When I'm not so busy," replied Mrs. Brown.

As Tommy backed out of the room, he too imagined playing with the moose by the tree, which, of course, couldn't happen until his mother finished making him.

Chapter 8

Back on the Tree

"Time for you two to go back to being ornaments on our Christmas tree," Tommy said as he picked up the angel and the soldier and ran down the hall to the living room. "Okay, Mom. Here they are."

Mrs. Brown pulled the small stepladder out from the hall closet and set it beside the evergreen giant. "Let's place the angel back on the top of the tree. What do you say, Tommy?"

"Remember, Mom? We didn't put her there last year. She climbed up during the night."

"Oh, that's right. Well, nothing wrong with giving her a helping hand this year. No sense me having to fix up those wings of hers."

Tommy agreed and climbed the three steps so he could once again reach up the tree as high as he could.

Mrs. Brown volunteered to do it instead, but he would have none of it. "She'll climb, Mother," he reminded her. "She'll get herself up the rest of the way." Tommy placed the delicate angel onto the tree and waited at the top of the ladder, but the angel did not move.

"Go ahead, Angel. We'll wait for you."

But the angel had not been on the tree in so long that she feared moving about, especially while the Brown family watched. She had grown accustomed to the role of guardian on Tommy's bike.

Reverting back to being an ornament might prove difficult, she worried.

"Tommy, why don't you hang the soldier next to her and worry about their final placement later."

"Okay, Mom."

"We should think of our tree as a work in progress. Change is a part of every life. It's good for us to expect it.

"Like when Jesus was born. Right, Mom? The whole world changed that night, didn't it?"

"Yes, Tommy. It sure did."

Tommy descended the stepladder and picked up the soldier by the string that was attached to the top of his head. Then he climbed back up the rungs and hung the soldier right beside his best friend, the angel.

When Tommy turned to go, the soldier took the angel by her hand, happy to be by her side once more.

Chapter 9

Sharing Emotions

"**H**ow do I get down from here?" wondered the moose. "This soft chair cushion beats frayed willow bark, but I don't want to stay up here forever. Maybe I could...?" He scooted his way to the edge of the chair. "I could grab hold of this spindle, wrap my leg around, and slide." As the moose spoke, he moved himself about. The next thing he knew—bang! His bottom hit bottom, and once again, he found himself in a new position.

"Well, what do you know about that?" he said. From there, he rolled his way, front to back, over to the basket and lifted himself up to assess the situation.

Laughter echoed down the hall from the room with the tree. The moose stilled himself to listen. "That is the most beautiful sound I have ever heard," he declared. "Even more beautiful than the song of the Whippoorwill outside the glass window." He listened some more. "Mrs. Brown and Tommy are enjoying themselves, but here I am, right back where I started, simply dreaming about a better life," said the moose.

Suddenly, out of nowhere, he began to hiccup, then wondered if it was time for another change to happen. "I want to be closer to the laughter," he said. "I want to see their faces when the laughter comes. Maybe if I lie on my side, I could roll myself to the doorway. If I can roll over front to back once, surely I can do it once times twenty."

The moose began to roll, front to back and back to front. After several revolutions, the moose could no longer tell the ceiling from the floor. It all melded into one blurry vision. The floor felt cold and hard, but he kept going.

Before he knew it, the moose had rolled himself out into the hall. He looked to his left and could see all the way down into Tommy's room. Then he looked to his right and could not believe his black, button eyes. There it was. The tree. The tall green tree and the stone fireplace and Tommy and the footstool and the opened ornament boxes.

The moose chuckled, then laughed with delight. Soon, laughter roared from deep within his belly. He had become a part of the joy others were feeling at the same time they were feeling it. The Browns and the moose were sharing joy together, and the moose no longer felt alone.

Chapter 10

Gifts of Good Cheer

A knock sounded on the front door.

"Can I get it, Mom?"

"Sure, Tommy."

He skipped over and swung open the heavy door. Standing on the welcome mat was Pastor Nelson holding a plate of freshly baked cookies. "Merry Christmas," he said as he presented the gingerbread.

"How you do this every year is beyond me," exclaimed Mrs. Brown. "Rushing around on Christmas Eve to each parishioner's household bearing gifts of good cheer."

The pastor smiled and noticed the finely decorated Christmas tree. "I see you placed the angel on the top."

Tommy and Mrs. Brown quickly looked, and there she was, perched like last year, on the very top of the tree, and she was smiling down at them, beaming white light.

"Has she blessed your home?" asked the pastor.

"Has she?!" exclaimed Mrs. Brown. "She's full of surprises, that one!"

"We put her on the tree, anywhere, and she climbs up the rest of the way," added Tommy.

"You don't say," said the pastor with a twinkle in his eye, as if he knew something important, and that important thing made him very happy inside.

"There's nothing she can't do," assured Tommy.

"Now, don't go getting too confident in just her and her alone," said the pastor. "It takes all the ornaments working together to accomplish great things."

Tommy looked back at the tree, and the soldier and the lamb and the wise king and the pirate and the clown, and he decided that the pastor had a good point. Their Christmas tree wouldn't be a Christmas tree if they only had the angel on top. Even the candles, when lit, would not seem as bright if all the individual ornaments weren't occupying their own special place on the tree.

"You're right, Pastor. We need them all, don't we?" said Tommy.

"We sure do. Each one plays an important role."

The moose listened from the hall, wishing he, too, could be valued.

"Pastor, can we offer you a hot cup of coffee before you go?" asked Mrs. Brown.

"I'm still working on the sermon for tonight's service."

"Tommy, you'd better bring the pastor a cup of coffee."

"Black, please," the pastor called to Tommy as he left the room.

"Do you always wait till the last minute?" asked Mrs. Brown.

"Not always. But I do always wait for the right words."

Mrs. Brown smiled. "Yes. Of course."

As Tommy walked quickly back to the living room, the dark liquid swayed back and forth in the cup, threatening to spill over the edges with every step.

"How's that paper route of yours going?" asked the pastor as Tommy handed him the cup.

"Great. I don't have to deliver any tomorrow, though. I get to sleep in."

"You? Sleep in on Christmas morning?!" said Mrs. Brown. "I'll believe that when I see it."

"I've asked Santa for a puppy dog this year."

"A puppy? That's quite a request."

Just then, Mr. Brown opened the front door, happy to be home early this Christmas Eve.

"Look who's here. Merry Christmas, Pastor."

"Merry Christmas, James."

The two men shook hands.

"Dropping off another ornament for our tree?" asked Mr. Brown.

"The wife baked cookies this year."

"They smell wonderful," added Mrs. Brown.

"I read in today's paper that President Roosevelt banned Christmas trees in the White House," said the pastor.

"Oh? Teddy's afraid of a fire, I suppose," added Mr. Brown.

"That can be a concern," agreed Mrs. Brown.

Tommy noticed the moose sitting alone in the hallway. He ran to him, picked him up, and carried him to the living room. Tommy waited again for a break in the conversation when he could speak.

"Well, that sermon isn't going to write itself," said the pastor. He took one last sip of his coffee. "We'll see you at this evening's service then?"

Mrs. Brown looked to Mr. Brown who nodded. "We'll be there."

The two men shook hands again as Tommy watched. Then, with one arm around the unfinished moose, the boy quickly jutted out his free hand, wanting to say goodbye as his father had.

Pastor Nelson took Tommy's hand and shook it hard. "We'll see this fine young man tonight as well."

"Thank your wife for the cookies," added Mrs. Brown.

"She loves to do it. See you soon." And out the door, Pastor Nelson went.

Tommy turned to his mother and father as they made their way down the hall to change. "Do you think Santa will bring me a puppy for Christmas?"

"You'll have to wait and see," said Mr. Brown.

"I've laid out your wool suit, son," said Mrs. Brown.

Tommy placed the moose on his back beneath the tree.

"Oh, Mom! Dad! We forgot to light the candles on the tree."

"We'll do it after dinner, son."

"I don't know how we forgot that. It's our favorite part," Tommy said as he ran down the hall to change his clothes.

Chapter 11

Made on Purpose

The moose could not believe his good fortune. Tommy had laid him down at the foot of the great tree on his back. He lay there looking up through the scented boughs. A handful of needles quietly fell on his chest. "Did you see that? Did anyone see that?" asked the moose.

"I saaaaaw it. What's the big deeeeal?" cried the lamb, not at all impressed.

"What's the big deal?" said the moose. "Something happened to me, and I didn't even have to move."

"You have quite an interesting way of looking at things," said the wise king. "Quite unique, I would say. Of course, it is known that many things happen in life without anyone ever doing anything to cause them."

The moose was delighted beyond belief. The ornaments could communicate with him, and valuable ideas could be exchanged. "I wish I were an ornament," blurted out the moose. "I wish I was like you."

"Caaaaareful what you wiiiiish for," said the lamb.

"If I were careful what I wished for, I would have nothing to do," said the moose. "I like wishing. For some, wishing is all they've got."

"I don't mean to burst your balloon," said the clown, "but why do you want to be something you're not? Seems like a big waste of time to me."

"You all have something important to do. You bring joy into this house. I don't do much of anything but sit in a basket all day."

The angel listened carefully from the top of the tree. "But how do you know?" she asked. "You're just getting started. Be patient and see what gets placed before you.

"I can jump," said the moose.

"Really?"

"Oh, yes. And I enjoy it. I jumped out of the basket where I lived my entire life. But what I want now is to hang on the tree like you. But I don't think I could attach a rope to the top of my head because my antlers are in the way."

"That is inconvenient," said the angel.

She knew that unless you listened, you couldn't truly know anyone. Listening, after all, is love. And the angel listened with such love that the moose's long-confined feelings were set free. He slumped over onto the hardwood floor and cried.

"Moose?" asked the angel.

"Yes?" He looked up at her pretty face, smiling down at him.

"There must be a reason why your antlers are there."

"Really? How do you know?"

"Because you were made on purpose, and the manner you were made was also on purpose. You'll have to be patient and wait to find out the reason."

The moose wasn't sure if patience was something he had or not, but he had gotten good at waiting. Using the forearm of his red plaid jacket, he wiped away the fresh tears from his face and laid back down beneath the great green tree.

Chapter 12

The Candles

The Browns returned to the room where the tree stood, dressed in their church clothes.

"Can I light the candles this year?" asked Tommy.

"If you're careful," said Mrs. Brown.

"I'll help you," said Mr. Brown.

While father and son lit each candle on the tree, Mrs. Brown gathered their winter coats and one of the pies from the kitchen and set the family Bible on the end table. She was anxious to see whether the pastor finished his sermon, though she knew he must have. Deadlines play an important role in getting something done, she thought. Maybe that's why she hadn't finished sewing the items in her basket.

"Okay. Ready, Mom."

Mrs. Brown crossed to the lantern sitting on the table and turned the knob on its side, causing the room to go dark.

The three of them stood gazing at the tree, which was lit up like the sky on a crystal-clear night. Quiet, still, and stunning in the Browns' little home on the hill, the tree gave them a sense of calm and beauty.

The moose was absolutely enchanted, looking up at something so dazzling yet tangible and real. The stars outside his window in the sewing room seemed so very far away and unreal. This light flickered directly before him, so close he could almost touch it.

"Silent night, holy night, all is calm, all is bright," the Brown family began to sing softly. The moose and all the ornaments listened in awe. "Round yon virgin, mother and child. Holy infant, so tender and mild. Sleep in heavenly peace. Sleep in heavenly peace."

"Wow! Fantastic!" said the moose out loud. He couldn't help himself. He didn't even think before he spoke. The happiness simply forced the words from his mouth.

"Did you say something?" asked Mr. Brown.

"No. You, Tommy?" asked Mrs. Brown.

"Nope. And I didn't hear a thing."

"Well, you two outdid yourselves this year," said Mr. Brown. "The tree is beautiful."

"Thank you," said Mrs. Brown, kissing her husband gently. "Glad to have you home so early on Christmas Eve."

Tommy noticing this tenderness, hoped that one day he would meet a good woman like his mother, and they would marry.

"What's this unmade moose doing lying on the ground?" asked Mrs. Brown.

"Oh, sorry. I'll put him back."

"Thank you."

"Want to blow out the candles on the tree, Mr. Brown?"

"Anything for you, Mrs. Brown."

Tommy's father extinguished the flame of each candle on the tree. The moose watched him carefully, finding it all so exciting. Mrs. Brown re-lit the lantern. Everyone working together inspired the moose.

The candles were placed low enough on the tree for Mr. Brown to blow them out without using the stepladder. He had only the mid-section of the tree left to go. As Mr. Brown drew closer, the moose saw the pirate ornament take a single step out in front of the last remaining flame.

"Tommy, put the moose away now."

The boy picked up the moose by the hand and walked down the hallway, back to the sewing room, back to the basket, back to prison.

"Wait! Wait, Tommy," cried the moose. "The pirate. The pirate on the tree."

It's difficult to predict when a child will lose that connection to the make-believe world, to the world of magic, where all things are possible. Sometimes, it happens slowly over months, and then sometimes, that special sensitivity can be lost all in one day. But regardless and for whatever reason, Tommy could no longer hear the moose, though he still loved him very much.

"Tommy! Tommy, the pirate, is blocking the light. Make sure your father blows out the candle behind the..."

Tommy dumped the moose into the sewing basket and left the room. The room suddenly became very dark, and the moose was frightened.

Tommy put on his galoshes, wool coat, and knit hat. Once they were all bundled, Mrs. Brown blew out the lantern's light, and they closed the front door behind them. The sound of the door closing was almost too much to bear.

Chapter 13

Silent Night

The moose listened to the silence as it echoed through the rooms of the Brown home. He looked out the window as the three dark figures disappeared down the hill and into the night. Maybe the other ornaments noticed the lit candle. Maybe they would do something. Certainly, the angel on the top of the tree would make sure they were all safe.

He tried to forget about it. It wasn't his problem. After all, he wasn't an ornament. He was an unmade moose. Nothing was ever expected of him.

Slowly, the smell of smoke slithered its way into the sewing room. The moose's acute nose sniffed. "Pine needles," he said. "The pine needles on the Christmas tree are burning. And all those ornaments are hanging on the tree!"

The moose looked down at his one leg. "I'm not finished. How can I help them? How can I do anything?" He then remembered something the angel said. She said that everyone was born with a purpose and for a reason, and if he were patient, maybe he'd find that reason. "Maybe this is why I was created," he thought. "Maybe being unmade doesn't matter. Maybe I already have everything I need to help the ornaments."

The moose quickly assessed his abilities. He could jump, not far, but certainly out of the basket.

He jumped up and over the edge of the basket, tripped, and fell to the ground. But he got back up. He knew how to fall now, so that's something he didn't have to be afraid of anymore.

In the room with the tree, the angel smelled something burning, too. She looked down and saw a tiny spark taking hold of a small section of the Christmas tree. Without hesitation, she cried out, "The tree's on fire. Someone, help us."

"There must be a faster way," said the moose. He stood up and it was then the idea struck him. He took those annoying sticks, placed one under each arm, and used them to balance himself. He worked fast, putting one stick out in front and then the other, making his way quickly out the door and into the hall.

The soldier spotted the moose from the top of the tree, "Help us, Moose," he cried. The angel grabbed hold of the soldier's hand as she watched the small fire dance its way up the front of the tree.

The pirate ornament tossed one end of the popcorn garland down from the tree, grabbed hold of it, and tried to descend as if it were the mast of a ship. Meanwhile, the moose hurried toward the tree as quickly as he could, using the knitting needles under his armpits like crutches.

The other ornaments did their best not to panic. Most of them were tightly attached to their branches, and they were confused about how to detach themselves.

The wise man understood the dilemma, but his arms were not long enough to reach the place where the string met with the branch. He strained desperately but failed to unhook himself.

"Angel, jump," said the soldier.

"I'm not going without you," she replied.

"You must. This time, you must. I'll get down, somehow."

When the moose arrived at the bottom of the tree, he realized he did not need two legs to climb. He immediately pulled himself up into the branches, pushing himself with his one leg. He could cover distances quicker because the moose was larger than the

ornaments. He reached the lamb and easily moved his thin arm through the boughs and slipped the lamb's string off of the branch, freeing him.

There wasn't enough time for the moose to climb down the tree with each ornament and then back up again to save the next, but he could think of no faster way.

"Haaaang me from your aaaantlers," said the lamb. "Your aaaaantlers!"

The moose quickly lifted the lamb above his head and secured the string into one of the dips of his antlers. He moved on to the terrified wise man, who knew more than anyone what lay ahead for them if they failed. The moose reached through some pine needles, plucked the purple ornament from the tree, and hung him safely on his rack.

When the moose came to the clown, there was no string on his head. Instead, the clown's hand tightly grasped a thin but sturdy branch.

"Let go," said the moose.

"No."

"You'll burn."

"I can't help it. I'm afraid," said the clown.

The moose looked up at the angel, and despite the dangerous situation they found themselves in, she was smiling at them, beaming white light.

"Clown?" the moose said.

"Yes."

"Look up at the angel."

The clown leaned back his head and looked to the top of the tree. There she was, a beacon of beauty, beaming at him.

"Don't be afraid," she said calmly. "Let go."

With his eyes fixed on the angel, the fear left him. The clown let go of the branch and grabbed hold of the moose's antlers, joining the others.

The moose searched the boughs for the pirate but couldn't find him. Just then, a camel appeared from behind the tree. He was advancing steadily but not fast enough. The moose grabbed hold of him, and onto his antlers he went.

"Why thank you," said the slow-speaking camel. "We sure appreciate what you're doing."

With no time for pleasantries, the moose asked, "Who are we missing?"

"The soldier," said the wise man.

"Heeeee's way up theeeeere with her," bleated the lamb.

Dry trees burn fast, and the moose wasn't moving fast enough. The climbing flame drew nearer by the second. The moose felt the heat nipping at his foot. Fear finally overtook him, and he froze, unable to make another step. "Hiccup." *Oh, not now,* thought the moose.

The angel had been watching and knew he needed encouragement. "Moose," she said softly, "you were made for this. You are a walking Christmas tree for those ornaments. Keep walking. Keep going. You're doing just fine."

Chapter 14

The Walking Christmas Tree

The idea of the moose being a *walking Christmas tree* made him smile so large his face could not contain the joy. Suddenly filled with such energy, there was no stopping him. In less than a second, the moose stood beside the soldier at the top of the tree and untied him while the angel held the soldier's hand.

"Jump now," said the solider to the angel, and up and onto the moose's rack he went. Once the angel knew the soldier would be safe, she leaped off the top of the tree, gracefully gliding over the inferno to the floor below.

Down the back of the tree, the moose climbed, but with all the ornaments dangling from his antlers, he couldn't see very well and grew more frightened by the minute. Suddenly, one of the clown's balloons popped, and they all jumped. The moose nearly lost his balance.

"You're too close to the fire," warned the clown as the moose continued to move downward.

Every time another balloon popped, they knew the flames were getting closer. Each ornament gave suggestions to aid in their escape, and at last, the moose descended the final limb onto that beloved hardwood floor.

He kneeled down before the angel who waited for them and lowered his antlers to the ground. The angel unattached each ornament, pulling their strings free from the moose's rack.

"Now we know what those antlers were for, don't we?" she asked. And for the first time, the moose felt very good about how he had been made and forgot all about his apparent incompleteness.

Just then, a call came from up inside the tree. "Lonely!" the voice cried out. The second call was louder than the first, "Lonely!"

The moose thought they had gotten everyone down. He counted the ornaments. They were all there. He looked to the angel.

"The pirate," she said.

"He's imporrrrrted," added the lamb.

The moose began to hiccup. If it hadn't been for the pirate, this Christmas tree fire never would have happened. The moose looked to the angel, who smiled at him. He knew what he must do. His hiccups stopped.

The moose took a deep breath and began to climb again. Up through the burnt twigs, he moved, under and over and between the charcoaled sticks. He followed the pirate's voice, who continued to call out a rather familiar word to the moose. "Lonely!" the pirate cried, prompting the moose to continue his ascent.

When the moose arrived, he seized the pirate, but he could not tug the small ornament loose. He twisted and turned and tugged some more, but something held the pirate prisoner.

"You're caught on something," said the moose. "What is it?" He used his nostrils to assess the situation. The moose smelled the glue of a sticker, located it, and rubbed the label off the pirate's foot with his nose. That solved the problem. He then shoved the twine up and over the pirate's little black shoe, finally pulling him free. It's then the moose noticed that the pirate had only one working leg, too. *Well, what about that?* he thought to himself. *I'm not so different after all.*

The moose looked downward in the direction of his newfound friends waiting below. But with all the smoke, he could no longer tell exactly where they were. He knew he had to go down but which way was down? The smoke billowed densely.

He thought back to the quiet of the sewing room when he rolled on the floor and watched how the ceiling and ground became the same. He couldn't tell, then either, which way was up and which was down. The smoke clogged his brain. Confusion stopped him, and for crying out loud, a sticker was stuck to the end of his nose!!!

The angel knew it was taking too long. On her flight down, she noticed the branches and the distances between them. She sensed the moose was frozen with fear. The soldier reached for her hand. The camel took the soldier's hand because he, too, knew something was wrong. The wise man put his hand on the camel's hump and his other hand on the lamb's head, and the clown, who had no more balloons to hold, completed the circle.

The angel began to pray, and the others joined in. Together, their prayer became a beacon so bright that even the smokiest haze could not obscure the light they radiated. With newfound vision and courage, the moose emerged from the flames to the cheering crowd that awaited him.

The moose dipped his rack to the ground, and the angel unthreaded the knot that tied the pirate to his antlers. She then pulled the label off the moose's nose and crumpled it up. "No need for this anymore."

The little fellow looked more frightened than all the other ornaments put together. As the label stated, he was not made here in this town or any nearby town, for that matter. The pirate did not speak their language. "Lonely!" was all he knew to say. Tears rolled down his cheeks.

He was sorry for stepping in front of the burning candle, a selfish move motivated by his intense fear of the dark. But how could he tell them that? How could they possibly understand?

No words could better express the disappointment and regret on the pirate's face. The angel understood these feelings. She, too, had suffered in a similar way, and by God's grace, she'd escaped the darkness of the storage box. Without hesitation, she embraced him.

Just then, Tommy stormed through the front door. "Holy cow!" He stood watching the room's ceiling grow black from the smoke and flames.

His mom and dad, still at church, had asked him to return to the house to retrieve another pie. And now, with his father's fears realized, their home would soon burn to the ground from the Christmas tree fire.

Tommy remembered what his father had told him so very many times. "If there's a fire, son, remember, I keep this fire extinguisher here, by the fireplace."

Tommy turned, and there it was. He picked it up and pointed it at the tree. When he pushed the lever, a foggy solution burst forth and blew the moose down the hall and clear into the kitchen.

"Hiccup."

Tommy tried again. He directed the spray first at the ceiling and then down the rest of the tree. In only a few moments, Tommy had extinguished every flame.

When Tommy saw that all the ornaments had made it safely off the tree, he asked, "How did you all manage to get down in time?" The ornaments stood there, pleased to see him but unsure how to explain what had just happened.

Tommy surveyed the charred black sticks and said, "I guess we don't have to take down the tree this year. I always hated that part, anyway."

The moose chuckled, then laughed from his belly. The joyful sound made the angel and the soldier laugh as well. Soon, the lamb, the wise man, and the camel joined in. The camel's laughter was slow, as expected, but it was hearty just the same.

Tommy could actually hear them all laughing, and he was thrilled to have his friends back in his life, so he joined in on the fun, too. He knew his parents would be pleased. Christmas could not have been better, whether he received the puppy or not.

The moose happily watched as everyone laughed together. Then he declared, "This is the most beautiful sound I've ever heard. I'm not lonely anymore." The pirate, recognizing the significance of the one word he knew, took the moose by the hand and smiled.

ABOUT CLIMBING ANGEL PUBLISHING

Climbing Angel Publishing was founded in 2015 to share stories of hope and encouragement, aid in the gathering together of the community, and support the process of betterment. The following books are available at your leading online bookstores.

ADULT BOOKS: (Romans 8:28-30)

In His Image by Sam Polson
(English, Romanian, Mandarin, & Spanish)
By Faith by Sam Polson (English & Romanian)
My Birthday Gift to Jesus by Lisa Soland
Without Ceasing by Dr. Dennis Davidson
SonLight: Daily Light from the Pages of God's Word by Sam Polson
Corona Victus: Conquering the Virus of Fear, Sam Polson
(English & Romanian)
Art Bushing: His Diary, Letters, & Photographs of WWII,
by Art Bushing
Art & Dotty: His Diary, Their Letters & Photographs of WWII,
by Art Bushing
Trimisul by Stan Johnson (Romanian)
Life Changing Prayer by Sam Polson
The Climbing Angel Christmas Treasury,
by a variety of authors
J. Calvin Coolidge: Letters from the Korean War
by J. Calvin Coolidge
Stories from Kingman, AZ: The Heart of Historic Route 66
by Loren B. Wilson
Pathways: Ancient Paths from the Pages of the Old Testament
by Sam Polson
Fear Not by Sam Polson

THE SINGLE SERMON SERIES: (1 Pet. 3:15)

Jesus is Alive! by Mike Sager
My Mother's Bible by Sam Polson
The Lost Boys by Jake Bishop
Melchizedek: A Shadow of Christ by Jerry Scheumann
A Servant of Christ by James Alan Lynch
Dreaming God's Dream by Dr. Al Cage
Resisting Sin by Colin Hughes
A Call to Christians by Chris Reed
Making Plans in God's Will by Joe Kappel

CHILDREN'S BOOKS: (Philippians 4:8)

The Christmas Tree Angel by Lisa Soland
The Unmade Moose by Lisa Soland
Thump by Lisa Soland
Somebunny To Love by Lisa Soland
(English & Mandarin)
The Truth About God's Rainbow by Lisa Soland
God's Promises by Lisa Soland
The Boy & The Bagel Necklace by Lisa Soland
God's Hands and Feet by Lisa Soland
I Like To Be Quiet by Joni Caldwell
Wheels Off! by Karlie Saumier
Ella's Trip of a Lifetime by Melanie Ewbank
Because You Are Mine by Gayle Childress Greene
Jeremy Plays the Blues by Amy Oden Simpson
Bad Hair Day by Jasmyne Simpkins
I Like To Read by Joni Caldwell
Trunks Up! by Karlie Saumier
Perusha's Paradise by Bette Reed Smith
Ruby and the Treasure Within
by Tonya Celeste Hobbs
Abby, the Wonder Dog & her Warrior Princess
by Melanie Ewbank
The Christmas Coat by Lisa Soland
Danger Around the Bend by Karlie Saumier
The Christmas Tree Moose by Lisa Soland